WINTER
CABOOSE

WINTER CABOOSE

A Sequel to *The Blue Caboose*

Dorothy Hamilton

Illustrated by James Converse

HERALD PRESS
Scottdale, Pennsylvania
Kitchener, Ontario
1983

Library of Congress Cataloging in Publication Data

Hamilton, Dorothy, 1906-
  Winter caboose.

  Summary: When Jody's father reappears, after
deserting the family soon after returning from Vietnam,
Jody begins to accept his reasons for leaving.
  [1. Family life—Fiction] I. Converse, James, ill.
II. Title.
PZ7.H18136Wh   1983   [Fic]   83-10816
ISBN 0-8361-3341-2

WINTER CABOOSE
Copyright © 1983 by Herald Press, Scottdale, Pa. 15683
   Published simultaneously in Canada by Herald Press,
   Kitchener, Ont. N2G 4M5
Library of Congress Catalog Card Number: 83-10816
International Standard Book Number: 0-8361-3341-2
Printed in the United States of America
Design by Alice B. Shetler

83 84 85 86 87 88 10 9 8 7 6 5 4 3 2 1

To my friend,
Kathleen Meehan

Chapter 1

JODY BRYANT sat on the edge of the mini-porch at the back of the Blue Caboose. His legs reached as far as the bottom step of the second chunk of railroad ties. *I guess Mom's right. Eleven may be my best growing year yet.*

He heard a truck chugging over the crushed stone of the driveway. He watched as it went past the end of his caboose home, on the way to the old factory. *That guy must have a real heavy load*, he thought. *The engine sounds out of breath.*

He was thinking about going over to the laundromat to meet his mother when Carlos Mendez came running from the mobile home across the drive.

"Hey, amigo," Carlos said. "What you doing?"

"Hey yourself. What's it look like I'm doing?"

Carlos grinned. "That *was* a dumb thing to say."

"I guess we all say dumb things sometimes. Anyway, do you have something you think both of us could do?"

"Maybe so, maybe not. You might not want to do what I'm thinking of. But that's bueno—okay."

"Try me. What do you have in mind?"

"Well, a lot more people are working at the factory now."

"I know. I counted nineteen cars in the parking lot," Jody said.

"I was thinking we might go over there and see what they're doing. Or have you?"

"No, I haven't been inside. Just at the back where trucks unload," Jody said. "Do you think we *could* go inside? I suppose we could ask."

"Si—that's what I thought," Carlos said. "If you want."

"Si—yes—I want. Wait until I check to see if the stove's okay—if I turned it off. And I'd better leave a note."

8

"You leave it burning all the time when it is colder," Carlos said.

"I know. Mom says we have to find another way to keep warm before real winter comes."

"You won't have to move to another house to keep warm, will you?"

"No, I think Mom will find a way here," he said as they headed out the door.

Jody led the way through the door of the factory. He thought as he looked around, *Carlos always wants to be last. Is it because he's a Chicano—a migrant kid—or just because he's Carlos?*

No one was in sight. The chair behind the wide desk was empty. "This place does not look old on the inside," Carlos whispered. "Why do we always say it is the *old* factory?"

"Because it is," Jody said. "And on the outside that's how it looks."

Jody walked toward a door at the back of the room. "This looks like an office," he said. "A typewriter and shelves and stuff."

"I hear pounding," Carlos said. "Are you scared to go back there?"

"A little, but we can't ask anyone if we—"

Before he could finish the sentence a man came through the door. "Well, good morning, gentlemen. Anything I can do for you?"

Carlos looked at Jody. "Well, we were wondering. Could we look around?" Jody asked.

"No reason why not. But first we should introduce ourselves. I'm Jim Hunter—and you are—"

"This is Carlos—Carlos Mendez. He lives in the mobile home over there. And I live in the caboose."

The man didn't say anything for what seemed like a long time. He scratched his head and glanced back into the factory. Jody couldn't think what might be wrong. Then he decided the man had heard something that needed to be done, like an engine stopping or making a funny noise.

"Let's see, where were we?" Jim Hunter said. "You were saying that you live in the Blue Caboose. That means your name is Bryant. Right?"

"Right. But how did you know that?"

"Let me see. How did I know that?" Mr. Hunter said. "Must be that Joe Gable mentioned the name. Yeah, that must be how I know."

He sure acts funny, Jody thought. *Probably because he has a lot on his mind.*

"You gentlemen wait here till I see if any dangerous machinery is running," Mr. Hunter said, "like saws. Then I'll take you on a guided tour."

"Maybe we should not have come," Carlos said.

Jody shrugged his shoulders. "The way Mr. Hunter acts is hard to understand. But grown-ups are kind of strange a lot of times."

"Ready?" Jim Hunter said as he came back to the office. As they walked along, Jody was surprised at all the different kinds of work being done. On one aisle four men were cutting boards

10

into four shapes—into rockers, legs, sides, and backs for small rocking chairs. Four women were putting them together farther down. Another eight people were working on wagons and others were making scooters. The smell of new wood and the whine of saws filled the air.

All at once the large room was still. "It's noon," Mr. Hunter explained.

"We'd better go," Jody said. "But thanks for showing us around."

"No problem," Jim Hunter said.

"I have a question," Jody said. "I see younger people here. I mean someone, Mr. Gable maybe, told us that retired people work here."

"They do. But business is booming and we're hiring some others who can't get jobs."

"Well, thanks again. Come on, Carlos."

"That was a bueno time," Carlos said as he followed Jody down the drive. "But that one guy in there. I think he knows you."

"You mean Mr. Hunter?"

"No, another one. The man on the ladder," Carlos said.

"I didn't see him. What makes you think he knows me?"

"Because, he came down a ladder when you were by yourself looking at a scooter. He looked right at you and then hurried back up the ladder."

"I didn't even see a ladder," Jody said. "That guy probably forgot something."

"Probably. I never thought of that."

As they walked toward the drive Jody said, "I guess I don't pay much attention to how people look at me, or even if they do."

"You might if you'd been a new kid as many times as I have. And *if* you—oh, forget it."

"You were going to say if I'd been born a Chicano. Do you still feel different from other people?"

"Not so much. At least not with some people, like you."

"Good. Say, it's getting cloudy and cooler. I'd better hurry home and turn up the heat. See you! *S-e-e,* not the *si* that means yes. Understand?"

"Si. See you."

Jody knew that his mother was at home before he opened the door. He heard music. He liked coming home to the caboose all the time but it was better when she was there.

"Hi. Did you get off early?"

"A little," his mother said. "Mr. Gable took over for the last half hour so I—or we—can go shopping."

"For food—or what?"

"Food *and* what—the what being an electric heater. I want to buy us one like the Gables have at their lake cottage."

"We're going to the shopping center, I guess."

"No, uptown. We can go by bus. And since it's Friday, the stores are open until nine. Do you want to go along?"

12

"Sure! After we eat?"

"I think we'll eat at the department store cafeteria. We might as well give ourselves a treat. Are you in favor of that?"

"I'm in favor," Jody said.

Chapter 2

"I'M GLAD the men who are running the factory put up the pole lights," Jody's mother said as they left the Blue Caboose.

"Because they shine way over here?"

"Yes. So far it's been daylight when we came home. Most of the time anyway. But the days are shorter now."

Does that mean she's afraid? Jody thought. *Does she wish we hadn't moved from Walnut*

14

Street? He felt a knot in his throat. A little one like he had when he'd wondered if his mother was worried because his dad had skipped out.

"Why are you so quiet?" his mother asked as they walked to the corner of Twelfth and Walnut to the bus stop.

"I guess I was doing what we said we'd not be doing anymore. Keeping something to myself," Jody said.

"Like am I sorry we moved? Like am I afraid where we live?"

"Mom! How'd you know?"

"You might be surprised how much mothers can see. Especially if we don't let ourselves forget how we felt when we were young."

The big city bus pulled up to the curb, the brakes hissed, and the door clanged.

After Jody and his mother found a seat halfway back he said, "These windows are funny. We couldn't see in but now we can see out. Why?"

"I don't really know. But going back to what we were talking about. I'm not sorry we moved. How about you?"

"No way."

"I just think we should be wise and careful. Besides, having the Mendez family across the drive makes me feel safer. Are there any other little worries buzzing around up there in your mind?"

"I don't hear any."

"Good. Or as Carlos says, 'Bueno.' "

Jody couldn't remember the last time he'd been downtown. "It's sort of nice down here," he said, "with cars not zipping around in all directions."

"You're right," his mother said. "On one-way streets you know which way to look for cars."

They went to the hardware store first. Jody listened part of the time while his mother talked to the salesman. He liked the glow and the warmth of the heaters. He could picture himself in bed watching the red coils of wire. Then he walked around and saw all kinds of tools and things like light cords and sockets. *There sure is a lot of stuff in this world,* he thought. *Who figured out how to make everything?*

He was looking through the top of a glass case at a tray of pocketknives. Something about them made him think of his dad. Before he could remember what, he heard his mother say, "I'll call you when I get things worked out. I'm almost sure I'll take the square heater. It'll fit in nicely where we are. Ready, Jody?"

"Ready for what?"

"Ready to go? Ready to eat?"

"Both." He had some questions in his mind but he wasn't in a big hurry to have them answered. He decided he was more hungry than curious.

"We'd better not stop to do any window shopping," his mother said. "The cafeteria closes at six."

"Why? Why would it close before the store?"

"Probably so people are not sitting around eat-

16

ing when those who work here are ready to go home."

Jody felt a little uncomfortable in this new place. *Everyone is either grown up, or real little kids*, he thought. *But I can still eat.*

"Look at the menu on the wall while we wait in line," his mother said. "Choose what you want before we pick up our trays."

Jody couldn't decide which he wanted most, fried chicken or barbecued beefburger. He decided to get the chicken because most of the time they ate in places where about all you could get was sandwiches.

He followed his mother to a table in the corner, being careful that his caramel-nut ice cream wouldn't tip over on the macaroni and cheese.

After he had eaten several bites he asked, "Do you think you'll buy one of the heaters we saw back there?"

"Yes, I do. The square one doesn't have to be in the middle of the room, so things near it won't get too hot. The round one does. We don't need much in the path as we move around."

"Do you feel real crowded in the caboose? Is that what you mean?"

"No, not as long as we keep things in order. I do miss a shower or tub. But people kept clean by taking sponge baths for years and years."

"And Mr. Gable lets us use the shower in the room behind the laundromat. Why is there a bathroom there anyway?"

17

"I don't know. I never thought to ask. But going back to the heater. The electric bill will be higher. And there's one other thing I haven't had a chance to discuss with you."

"Something good?"

"Something good." Jody's mother broke a fluffy biscuit in half before she went on. "I received some money from your father in the mail today. It was more than enough to pay for the heater."

"Is that a lot?"

"Quite a lot."

"Then Dad must be doing okay. He must be proving that he can hold down a job."

"Yes, it seems so. He sent a note along, too. He said he'd heard we were getting along okay."

"Who do you think told him that?"

"I don't know. But he does have friends from around here. Someone might have seen him somewhere. Or he could be writing to them."

Other questions came to Jody's mind. *Only it's really the same one over. If Dad proves he can hold a job, will he come back? How would that be?* He didn't tell his mother what he was thinking this time. *After all we've talked about this before. Mom doesn't know any more than I do, or she would've told me.*

The wind took their breath away. Jody and his mother stood with their backs to the north as they waited for the bus.

18

"One thing does puzzle me about this letter," she told Jody. "It came to the laundromat in care of Mr. Gable."

"Could you tell where it was mailed?" Jody asked.

"No, the postmark was smudged. But that's enough about that. Have you had all you want to eat?"

"You know something? I have. That's really weird," Jody said. "I thought I'd never get enough."

"That's not so weird. After all stomachs are only so big. I used to wish I knew exactly how large yours was—that I had a picture of it."

"Wow! That's weird. Why?"

"Well, I was new at being a mother. I worried a lot if you were getting enough to eat. I probably overstuffed you."

Before they left the department store they bought Jody a pair of gray jeans and two T-shirts, one blue and one red with white stripes.

The wind was strong. It took their breath as they went through the revolving doors. They stood with their backs to the north as they waited for the bus. Jody's mother said she wasn't making up her mind how to heat the caboose any too soon.

They'd left a lamp on and Jody could see its light in the window as they walked on the stone-covered drive and then across the grass to the Blue Caboose.

"It's warm in here," he said as he shut the door behind them.

"I know. It's windy but not nearly freezing outside."

The wind was the only outside noise Jody heard after he was in bed. It was all around them. *Like my blanket's around me in here. But I'm not afraid.* He remembered that Carlos said the mobile home shook a little in the storms. *It's like it breathes in and out.*

Jody raised up on one elbow. His mother was reading by the light of the lamp with roses on the shade. "I guess it'd take a real strong wind to tip this caboose over. Right?"

"Yes, but it's been here a long time. So, feel safe."

"I do, Mom."

Chapter 3

BY THE END of the next week the cream-colored electric heater had been delivered to the Blue Caboose. Mr. Gable brought it one afternoon after Jody came home from school.

That's probably Carlos, Jody thought when he heard the knock at the door. *I wonder what he wants.* He put the slice of bread down before he spread the glob of peanut butter. He almost said, "Come in, the door's not locked." But he remembered that his mother had said not to open the door, or tell anyone to come in, until he knew who was outside. About a hundred times she said that.

"Howdy, young sprout," Mr. Gable said. "I'm the personal trucker for this family at the moment."

"Oh, that's the heater. Come on in. I'll hold the door."

"I told your mama I'd get this thing going. If you want to give me a hand you can bring the laundry your mom sent over with me. Only it might take two."

"Take two what?" Jody asked.

"Two hands."

Within a few minutes the burner was glowing. Jody could feel warm air on his legs. Mr. Gable explained about shutting it off. "But starting it should be left to your mama, unless she says you can do it."

"Does she know how?"

"It's simple. I took this heater over to the Swish and Slosh and showed her the *high* and *low* and *off* settings. I gave a real demonstration. Besides, here's a book of instructions."

"I like the way you say things," Jody said, "like calling the laundromat the Swish and Slosh. Except why do you call me a young *sprout?* Sprouts aren't very important to anyone, are they?"

"That's the way I see life, I guess. Everything grows from a seed or a sprout. That's what we all

23

were once. Without the seeds and the sprouts coming on, this old world would be a sorry place. That's enough of my chattering. I'll be going. See you."

Jody finished spreading peanut butter over his bread. *It got a little dried out while Mr. Gable was here,* he thought. *But it's not too bad to eat.*

Carlos came to the door as Jody opened his math book. "I guess you're busy."

"I can quit. Why, do you want to do something?"

"Well, we could watch TV together or play my baseball game."

"Okay."

"Okay what?"

"Okay for baseball. I can watch TV at home."

The boys took turns spinning the arrow and moving players the number of spaces shown. While Carlos was waiting for Jody to move he said, "I wish my mama would try to learn to speak English."

"Why?" Jody asked. "Do you get tired of using Spanish words?"

"No. Only it would be bueno in school for my sister and me if we always talked in English. I could learn better."

"You do okay."

"Maybe. But it is not so easy. In many ways it is hard for all of us, and for Mama." Carlos explained that since the migrants had gone back to Florida and Texas for the winter the Mendez family had no visitors. "Mama is shy or maybe even ashamed. So she says it is best if no one comes."

"Even me?"

"That is what I want to tell you. She says it is hard for you because you try to talk and still you know she can't understand. She says all the time all she does is smile."

"Then I shouldn't come."

"No. What I'm trying to say is don't try to talk. She likes for you to be there. All the time she asks about you and says she should make the nut cakes you like."

"So! What's the big problem? Why didn't you just come out and say what you were thinking?"

"Because of the language. Thinking in Spanish and speaking in English doesn't always work. What I mean is not always like what I say."

"I got your meaning. I might even come over tonight, if Mom says it's okay."

"Bueno. I have some games and a TV. Adios."

"See you."

Jody had worked three rows of math problems when his mother came home. He didn't see why he had to do twenty long divisions, two more rows. If he knew how to do one right, that should be enough. Did all that practicing make him any better?

"So the heater arrived," Jody's mother said as she hung her coat behind the curtain at the end of the caboose. "It's nice and warm in here."

"It sure is. How come you're carrying books?"

"Oh, they're the account books for the laundromat. When Mr. Gable heard that I'd been to business college he turned them over to me. And he'll pay me overtime wages. Every little bit helps."

"Are we about out of money or something?"

"No, we're doing fine. But the heater will make our electric bills higher and we'll want to have a good Christmas."

"Christmas. I hadn't even thought about that. Will we have a tree?"

"A little one. And I've been thinking we might decorate the mini-porch. We could put lights around the railing and maybe the doorway. Well, what shall I make for supper?"

"I baked the potatoes—like you said."

They ate the potatoes with cheese Jody's mother had melted over the top, and ham salad sandwiches, and peaches for dessert.

"This is a good night for hot chocolate. Or would it be better before we go to sleep?"

"Let's wait," his mother said.

Jody shared what Carlos had said about his mother.

"She must be very lonely. And I can't think of one thing I can do to help her."

**Jody saw something move in the direction
of the factory. His heart beat a
little faster. Who could it be?**

"But you're going to try to think of something," Jody said. "I can tell."

Jody picked up a library book and then he remembered that he'd told Carlos he might go to his house. "Is it okay if I go see Carlos, Mom? Or is it not?"

"Well, I have no objections. But it gets dark so early. I don't like the idea of you being out after dark."

"But there's the big light."

"True. I tell you what. I'll stand outside and when you get there you turn a light on and off three times. And leave promptly at eight. I'll be watching."

Jody was getting sleepy when he started home. He yawned as he crossed the driveway. Then he saw something move in the direction of the factory. His heart beat a little faster. Who could it be? Some of the kids who messed around a lot? Were they looking for trouble?

Jody stopped. He could hear the crunch of footsteps on the crushed stone. Then the person, whoever he was, passed through the edge of the circle of light from the pole lamp. It was a man. Either he was wearing a heavy coat or he was a big person. A cap of some kind was pulled down over his ears.

"Jody," his mother called from the end of the Blue Caboose. "Is anything wrong?"

As he hurried to meet her, he decided not to

say anything about whoever was in the factory lot. No use to get her worried.

"Did you see that man?" his mother asked as they stepped up on the mini-porch. "Is that why you stopped?"

"Yes. Do you think he's supposed to be here?"

"Probably he works late. Or it could be the new night watchman. I think I heard Mr. Gable say something about hiring one."

Two orange mugs of chocolate were sitting on top of the new heater. Melting marshmallows floated like white islands in a chocolate sea.

"This is a good way to end a day," Jody said as he sipped, then licked the stickiness from his upper lip.

"A good way to end a good day. Right, Jody?"

"Right, mom."

Chapter 4

AS JODY turned down the soft blanket of his bed he asked, "Will you leave the new heater on all night?"

"Probably not. It's not that cold. We'll save that for the windy and below freezing times."

"Will we ever get snowed in over here, do you think?" Jody asked.

"We might. But we won't be alone. The Mendez family is here and people will either be at the factory or trying to get to it. But I'll store up some extra food. So don't worry."

"I wasn't *worrying*, Mom. I was just thinking it would be fun to be here and not have to go to school."

"I thought you liked school."

Jody turned over and stared at the blue ceiling before he answered. "I *do* like it," he said. "But it seems like everyone's supposed to *say* they don't."

"Why?"

"Because everyone's supposed *not* to like it. That's sort of dumb. Anyway, good night, Mom."

Jody turned on his side and watched the glow of the electric heater. It was so still in the Blue Caboose that he could hear the scratching sound of his mother's pen. His eyelids kept closing and he thought, as he had many times before, *I need props to keep them open.* Then he wondered why he was trying to stay awake. It was like some thought was coming closer and closer. *What am I remembering? Almost anyway?*

All at once he sat up in bed so fast that the springs bounced and pinged. "Mom," he said, "I'm about to remember something, I think. About Dad."

"Oh, Jody. Don't get yourself upset. Not at bedtime."

"I'm not upset. It's like looking at the new heater is reminding me of something. Some faraway time. Some other place."

31

Jody's mother walked over and sat on the edge of his bed. She rubbed one of his feet, then the other, with her fingers—something she'd done often when his father first came home from Vietnam. There was lots of loud talk and other noises to keep everyone awake then.

"It's the heater that's helping me remember whatever it is I can't quite think of yet. Mom, did Dad ever make me something with a knife? I mean whittle something?"

His mother started to shake her head. Then she said, "Oh yes. He did. Before he went to Vietnam. Before he reenlisted."

Jody wanted to stop and ask another question. He didn't know his dad had enlisted. He thought someone made him go into the army. *Why did he enlist? But I'll find that out later, if I want to.*

"We camped out for three days in a rented tent. You were only four years old," his mother said. "It was a good time and a sad time, a time of mixed feelings."

She told Jody that they'd sat around the campfire the last evening. "We were near a stream out east of town on a farm owned by someone your father knew." She said that the fire burned brightly and that Jody ate toasted marshmallows until his mouth and chin were sticky and he drank two cups of water.

"All that time Barney was whittling on a piece of wood. He must have brought it with him for a reason. I never thought about that until this very minute. How he happened to have the wood, I mean."

Jody heard what his mother was saying but another thought was in his mind. *Mom hasn't said my dad's name for a long, long time. She's just called him "your father" or "your dad."*

"He worked and worked," Lillian Bryant said. "You kept asking what he was making. But he wouldn't tell. He just kept saying, 'Watch. You'll see what will come out of this chunk of wood pretty soon.' "

"What did he mean by that?"

"Well, I suppose what he meant to make was in his mind, and with his knife and his hands it would sooner or later be seen."

"What was it?" Jody asked. Then he stopped. "I know what it was. I think I do. It was a little bird cage, with a bird inside that couldn't get out unless the bars were broken."

"That's exactly what he was making. Poor Barney. After he came home he was like that wooden bird in some ways."

"Did we lose the little cage? Did I?"

"No. It's in a box under the bed. After Barney came home from the war, then left again, I put it away. Being reminded of better times hurt—then it did. Now, are you ready to go to sleep?"

"I am. And as you always say, we'd better—"

"Better end this day so we can start another."

Before Jody's eyelids became heavy again he remembered being in the hardware store. *That's probably what I was almost remembering when I saw the knives in the glass case. It seems like things come back to us in pieces. Like parts of a puzzle. Like Dad using a knife while I looked at a fire.*

For the first time he didn't push thoughts of his father out of his mind. It was like the hurt was not as bad. Mostly his memories of his dad had been of the time when he came home and couldn't find a job and the money he had from being in the army didn't pay for everything. *Now there is a better picture in my mind—a little better one.*

He tried to imagine how it would be if there would ever be three people in his family again instead of two. *Dad's been away almost as much of my life as he's been here. It might not be easy to get used to having him around. Besides, it'd be crowded in here.*

The next thing Jody knew his mother was tugging on one of his ears, her wake-up signal. He blinked as he opened his eyes. "Is it late?"

"No, but it's time to get up. You're going to be surprised when you look outside."

"It snowed."

"How did you guess?"

"What else could it be? Wow! It really did—a lot! Will we get snowed in?"

"I doubt it. There's no wind, so there'll be no drifts. Sorry. Besides, I'm not prepared."

While Jody ate scrambled eggs and toast, his

mother made a list and talked about plans. She asked Jody to stop by the laundromat on the way home from school. "I'll need an extra pair of arms to carry home extra food."

"Carlos would help. Want me to ask him?"

"Fine. But let his mother know if it makes him late."

Before Jody dug his boots from the box under his bed, Carlos came to the door. "This is a bueno snow," he said. "Look outside. My papa went out after he was up and already he has made a path for us with the wheels of his truck."

"You like this snow, Carlos?" Lillian Bryant asked.

"Si, si. But my mama will not say it is good. All the time she says that the cold makes her stiff, like her legs are made of iron."

The snow was soft and wet, and Jody and Carlos took time to roll three balls of different sizes. They stacked them to make a snowman. "Only it is so small I think we have made a *snow boy*," Carlos said.

"We'd better hurry," Jody said. "The school bus from the other side of town is coming up the street. We might make a snow *man* tonight. If the snow doesn't melt or get so it won't roll. Besides, I might have to help Mom carry stuff home."

"This will not be the only snow this winter. Is that not so?"

"That is so."

Chapter 5

MOST OF THE SNOW was gone by the time
school was out. Pale winter sunshine had melted
all of it from the streets. Patches of white lay on
the grass, in the shade of houses, and near bushes
and trees.

"We will not go sledding this night," Carlos
said as he walked with Jody.

"Do you have a sled?"

"Si. My papa was to buy one today. He says

that if we are in the North we should do what there is to do here."

"You mean you've never gone sledding?"

"How could I? With no snow?"

"Well, I just never thought about that. I can't imagine living where there is no snow."

"I know. Like I couldn't see how it would be here."

"Can you go with me? I mean, it won't be fun carrying stuff."

"I'd like to help. My mama will worry if I'm late, but I'll hurry back if I can."

"Okay. See you."

Jody helped his mother in the laundromat until five o'clock, her regular quitting time. He emptied the waste cans which were almost as high as he was tall. He stacked small boxes in slots in the vending machines on the wall. He looked at each name, knowing that people wouldn't want to get a box of bleach for their coins when they'd pulled the lever under the name of a soap powder. He pushed the wide floor brush over the tan tiles, going around people's feet and clothes baskets. All the time he heard the rumbling-tumbling of dryers and, as Mr. Gable said, the swishing-and-the-sloshing of the washers.

"It's dark already," Jody said as he followed his mother to the sidewalk. "Would you, will you, be afraid to come to the caboose by yourself?"

"Mr. Gable talked to me about that this morning. He offered to have someone who works for him take me home. But I'd rather not bother people. Besides, there's no telling when the truck would be here. And Mrs. Gable doesn't drive at all, not even in the summer. So I'm going to come to work a half hour earlier and get off that much sooner."

When they entered the store, Jody's mother tore a part of her list from the rest and gave it to him. "You gather up what's on there, and I'll do the same with this part."

"Stocking up, I guess," Mr. Gable said, coming from behind the meat counter.

"Some. Snow makes us like squirrels," Lillian Bryant said. "Storing up for the winter."

"Only one thing's different," Mr. Gable said. "The bushy-tails get all that done before the snow flies."

As Jody reached for a box of baking soda he thought, *How do the birds and animals know when to do what? Squirrels store nuts for the winter. Birds build nests in the springtime and fly south in the winter. How do they know?*

Then Mr. Gable seemed to answer Jody's question, one he hadn't asked out loud. "Seems like nature's creatures use their way of knowing things better than we do. We depend on ourselves more and don't always listen to the signals we were born to hear."

"That sounds deep and wise to me," Lillian Bryant said.

"Don't give me the credit," the tall storekeeper said. "My granddad taught me that. I just passed it along."

As Mr. Gable pushed the buttons on the cash register he said, "You'd better take this home in one of the grocery carts. It might be a little bumpy, but you won't be losing Great Northern beans or potatoes and such all along the way. Better yet, I could bring it over after closing time."

"Thank you, but the cart will be fine," Lillian Bryant said. "Ready, Jody?"

"Ready."

Halfway up the crushed stone driveway Jody said, "Wait a minute. I have an idea of a way to help." He unzipped his brown and gold jacket and pulled his belt from the loops around the waist of his jeans. Then he looped the strip of leather around the top wire at the front of the grocery cart. "Now," he said, "I can pull."

As they reached the steps at the side of the mini-porch Jody said, "You know what I remembered, Mom? Sergeant Preston and his dog."

"You mean going over the snow, and the mounted policeman yelling, 'Mush.' "

"Right. I sure loved that show. I could watch it over and over."

"Well, King—that was the sergeant's dog, wasn't it? Mush!"

As Jody unhooked his belt and walked to the cart to pick up a sack of groceries he said, "Mom, something's different. What I'm walking on I mean. It feels like straw."

"I thought I noticed something," his mother said. "The pole light doesn't shine brightly on this side of the caboose. I'll get the flashlight after we unload this dogsled on wheels."

Jody followed his mother down the steps they'd made from chunks of railroad ties. He watched as she moved the flashlight above the ground. "There *is* straw here," she said. "And look, something else is different. See? Boards have been put up all around the caboose. You can't see the wheels. Who—"

"Mr. Gable? Would he do something like this? Why?"

"Oh, I know the why. It's to keep the wind from blowing underneath. The caboose will be easier to heat this way."

"But the straw—why is it here?"

"I have a feeling that—here, you look while I shine this light between the cracks at the end." Jody stooped and all he could see was squares or chunks of straw.

"It is straw. That is what you thought. Right? That it would be underneath?"

"Right."

"Look," Jody's mother said. "Boards have been put up all around the caboose. You can't see the wheels."

Jody followed his mother into the caboose asking, "Would Mr. Gable do this or have it done without saying anything to you or me?"

"Yes, I think it's exactly what he would do. I'll ask him and watch his face. I'll be able to tell if he is telling the truth."

"You think he lies?"

"Well—he might try to act like he didn't know what I'm talking about. But I'll want to pay whoever did this for us."

Jody helped his mother put away the groceries. "We don't have room for much more stuff," he said. "I'm stacking cans on top of cans now."

"I know what you mean," his mother said. "I had to wedge ground beef between ice cream and hot dogs. But I feel safer."

"These groceries must have cost a whole bunch of money."

"Oh, I forgot to tell you. Another check came today—from your dad. Mr. Gable cashed it for me."

"One just came."

"I know. This one was for only twenty-five dollars. But it paid for what we hauled home tonight."

"I guess Dad must still be proving he can hold down a job."

"Must be. Now, what shall we have for supper? Any choices?"

"Mom, we've got a lot of choices. How about spaghetti?"

"Good suggestion. I can make some garlic butter for our rolls."

Mr. Mendez came to the door while they were eating, and Jody asked him to come in and sit down.

"I will stand," Mr. Mendez said. He twisted his wide-brimmed hat around in his hands as he talked. The metal ends of the cord, which was twisted around the crown of the hat, flipped and clicked.

"Senora," he said, "we, my family and myself, want to be of help to you. Take you places if you have the need to go. Bring things."

"Well, that's so kind of you," Lillian Bryant said.

"The kindness goes two ways. So do not forget we are here to help you."

"Again, thank you. Before you go, did you see anyone putting straw under the caboose and boards around it?"

"I did not. But the missus—my wife—says some men were here."

"She didn't know them?"

"No, Cherita does not know many people here. Only a few. It is not so easy for her."

Chapter 6

"PEOPLE are so kind," Jody's mother said as she scraped spaghetti sauce from the plates. "Many are at least. Mr. Gable and now Carlos' father is offering to help."

"But you didn't let them do anything, Mom."

"I know. I have this strong feeling in me that if Barney did not want to be here to take care of us I shouldn't expect anyone else to help us."

"Are you still kind of mad at Dad?" Jody asked.

His mother smiled and reached over and ruffled his hair. "You don't like for people to be angry with each other do you?"

"Or with me."

"Going back to your question. I was angry or mad, as you say, resentful and hurt at first. But now I see that this time has been good for me." As she washed dishes she explained to Jody that she felt better about herself than she had in a long, long time. "I've found work, and I think I do a good job. It's really good to be able to depend on yourself. Not that I'm not grateful to people who care about us."

"You mean like Mr. Gable for using straw and boards to make the caboose warmer?" Jody said.

"If that's who did it."

Before Jody could ask who else would have made their caboose home safer from winter's cold, he heard a knock on the door.

Only it's more like a bumping, he thought.

"I'll see who it is," Jody's mother said. "Oh, hello. You're—let's see—you're Tim. Tim Afton, Right?"

"Yes'm. I'm Tim. Hi, Jody."

"Is something wrong? You're breathing hard."

"I know. I ran all the way."

Tim sat down on the chair Lillian Bryant pulled out from the table.

"It's that Tony," Tim said. "You might know who did it."

"Did what?"

45

"Let the air out of the tire on Mr. Mendez's truck."

"Were you with Tony when he did it?"

"No. I don't hang around with him and the twins. But I saw him and he knows I did."

"Why did you come tell us? It's fine that you're here," Lillian Bryant said, "but your home is closer."

"A lot closer. But the thing is, my mom's real good friends with Tony's mom. They'd never believe the mean stuff he does."

"Have you tried to tell your parents?"

"Well, ny dad's not home now. He's looking for a job. And Mom can't see what Tony really is. He's good at fooling people, at putting on a big act."

"So you're having a hard time staying away from Tony?"

"I sure am. I have to act like I'm studying a lot. And sometimes I do. Anyway, I needed to be away from over there. And this is the first place I thought of."

"I'm glad you came," Lillian Bryant said. "Take off your jacket and I'll make us some hot chocolate."

"Is it okay with you, Jody, if I stay?" Tim asked.

"Sure. We can watch TV maybe."

Jody's mind was full of a mixture of thoughts. He believed Tim was telling the truth about not being in the same trouble as Tony. Jody couldn't remember the two boys being together lately, but he hadn't really noticed that they were apart. *I guess I haven't been too friendly with Tim. And he needed another friend.*

Tim stayed until nine o'clock. When he said he should head home Lillian Bryant said, "Get your coat, Jody. We'll walk with Tim."

"You don't need to go with me, Mrs. Bryant. I'm not that scared. And I'm a pretty fast runner."

"Don't worry. I have something to ask Mr. Gable. We don't have a telephone."

Jody knew what his mother wanted to say to Mr. Gable. *But she doesn't need to ask him about the straw and the boards tonight. She's worried about Tim.*

After Tim ran up the steps to his apartment home, the two members of the Bryant family crossed the street and rang the Gable's doorbell.

"They're not at home," Jody's mother said. "I was almost sure they wouldn't be."

"Mom! That's sneaky."

"I know. Nice kind of sneaky though, don't you think?"

"I guess."

"It's late, I know. Your bedtime. But I felt sorry for Tim."

"Me too. Maybe he needs someone to be friendly to him."

"You have more or less stayed with Carlos, haven't you?"

47

"But Carlos needed someone too. I mean Tony and those guys didn't treat him right."

"Tim too?"

"Well, Tim sort of always hung back," Jody said.

"But now he's trying to break away completely. We'll think about this to see if there's a way to help. But now we're going to move furniture."

"Move furniture? At bedtime?"

"It won't take long," his mother said. She explained that there was more room in the caboose than she'd thought. "You have to live in a place for a while before you know how you want things. We can move your bed up to this side—about half way—and put mine across the end."

"I see one good thing about that. We won't have to climb over the end of a bed to get to our clothes and the trainmen's mini-bath."

"Right. And we can use your bed as a sofa. I love sofas with lots and lots of pillows. Of course I only have two now. Grab an end."

Jody sat down on his bed which was now a part-time sofa and looked around. "This is better. But maybe you won't be able to keep warm down there in real cold weather."

"Then we'll move the electric heater toward the middle."

"This way I can watch it without my neck being crooked."

Jody was in bed before his mother came from

behind the curtain. She sat down on her bed and rolled her hair up on fat pink curlers. Jody didn't see how she could sleep on the bumps.

He was getting sleepy but he said, "Mom, is it too early to talk about Christmas?"

"You mean like we used to do? No, I don't think so. It's not quite a month away."

As they talked Jody wondered why this was a special thing for them. They almost always remembered the same things. Jody said every year that his favorite tree ornament was the little gold angel that stood in a ring of silver. And he and his mother had always agreed that "Silent Night" was their favorite song. "Silver Bells" and "White Christmas" were second and third.

Jody's mother told Jody, as she had every year since he could remember, about the way she and her sister had decorated their tree with popcorn and cranberries strung in ropes when she was a little girl. "We didn't have tinsel or electric lights."

"Could we trim our tree that way? Only I'd like lights."

"We could. It'd be nice if we could get strings with one red and one white bulb all the way around, to go with the cranberries and popcorn. Now, good night."

Jody doubled his pillow and pulled the blanket over his shoulders. He kept seeing pictures of other Christmases in his mind. One year his big gift was a set of Lincoln Logs. He couldn't remember how many things he had built with them. He tried to think which was the very best gift he'd ever received. The transistor radio from last year was great and he still had the small car track and three racers. *I don't know what will be special this year*, he thought. *I'd better think of something. Mom might ask.*

He turned over and looked back toward his mother's bed. He could see that her eyes were open. "Hey, Mom. Did Dad ever talk about Christmas with us?"

"Not for a long time. Not since the war. Mostly he just smiled when he heard us talk about what was good."

Jody tried to remember how his father looked when he smiled. *A lot of the time I can't remember him at all*, Jody thought. *It's like he's farther and farther away.*

He raised up on one elbow and said, "Good night, Mom,"

Chapter 7

TWO SNOWS came during the next week. The first one was a white powdering that melted when the pale winter sun was overhead. The next one began when school left out on Friday afternoon. Big soft flakes fell on Jody and Carlos as they walked across Walnut Street and up the crushed stone driveway.

"This is not bueno," Carlos said.

"What do you mean? You've been talking about

wanting to try out your new sled. You said you were hoping it would snow."

"That is true. And that will be good. But if we are to be snowed in it would be better while it is schooltime."

"I see. But town kids don't get out much on account of bad weather. And it'd have to be terrible for buses not to get around in the city."

"That must be true," Carlos said. "Anyway, if much snow comes do you want to help try out my new sled?"

"I sure do. See you!"

Jody put his books in his cardboard storage box under his bed. He could almost hear his mother say, "The smaller the place, the neater we have to be. Clutter piles up quicker."

Jody took a banana from the wooden bowl on the table and turned on the television. At the bottom right corner of the screen he saw the words *Winter Storm Watch*. He thought, *"Watch" means maybe, "warning" means almost for sure. But they're not always right either way.*

He'd eaten half the banana when he decided that he should have gone to the laundromat. His mother hadn't said he should. *If it's going to snow a lot, she might bring home more food. But I don't know what we'll do with it—except eat it.*

He'd looked out the window three times before his mother came to the caboose. The ground was covered and the snow was a thick curtain in the air. He couldn't see the factory or any of the cars that were parked over there. The bushes at the back of the part of the lot which Jody had mowed in the summer were already whiskery white.

The third time Jody looked outside he saw a man walk away from the Blue Caboose, turn, and head toward the factory. *What would anyone be doing over here? Not jogging or out walking on a night like this surely.* He wondered if it was someone who left sale bills at doors and on car windshields. Sometimes Mr. Gable paid people to take these things around. Like when he was having a sale on pork chops or soda crackers or soap powder. *Mom says he does it mostly to give people work.*

Jody opened the door but didn't see any paper. If the man had left anything, it had blown away or was covered with snow.

As he turned he saw his mother coming through the curtain of snow. Someone was behind her. He hurried down the steps to take one plastic bag and saw that Tim was carrying a thin bumpy sack. "How come you're bringing things to eat in trash bags?"

"Go on in. You're not wearing a coat. Then we'll explain."

Lillian Bryant shook snow from her scarf and sat down to unbuckle her boots. "The plastic is to keep the groceries dry. This snow is wet. Brown paper would have been soggy by now."

"I could've helped."

"I know. This snow took me by surprise.

53

Besides, Tim came to my rescue. Want to stay and eat with us, Tim? Or would you rather go home and get out of this messy weather before dark?"

"Oh, this weather's okay with me," Tim said. "It's why I'm here. Carlos said to come over and go sledding if enough snow fell. Could be this is enough. Think so?"

"For you enough to go sledding," Lillian Bryant said. "For me too much. Already too much."

"Do you want to come too, Jody?" Tim asked. "Carlos wouldn't care."

"I know. I might come later. But don't wait for me."

"Don't go far, Tim," Mrs. Bryant said. "It'd be easy to get lost in this."

"We'll probably just go to that hill behind the factory. That's what Carlos said."

After Tim left, Jody said, "I guess those two are getting to be friends by themselves. They don't need me to do it for them."

"Are you feeling a little left out?"

"No. I could go. Carlos asked me to."

"Do you want to go?"

"Not really," Jody said. "Not while it's snowing this hard. I like to see where I'm going. And what I don't want to slide into."

"Well, I'm glad in a way. I have something to tell you."

"Good or bad?"

"Good—I hope. Not bad. At least it doesn't look bad now."

"Mom, that's mixed up. I don't know if I want to hear this or not."

Jody's mother unwrapped a package of fresh sausage links after she'd washed her hands. She began to talk as she lined them in a frying pan. "I heard from your father again today. Another of those letters came to Mr. Gable with the postmark blurred so I couldn't read it."

"Did he send more money?"

"No, not this time. This is the part I want to tell you. I *must* tell you. Jody, he's coming back."

Jody rested his cheek on a doubled fist and looked out the window. All he saw was snow. He didn't know what to say.

"How do you feel about the idea of your father coming home?"

"I don't know, Mom. How can I? I mean if it's going to be like I remember it—well—"

"I know. I have much the same feeling. But I have good memories too. More than you can have."

Jody's mother talked as she grated cheese into a creamy macaroni mixture. "He wrote a long letter. Before now it's just been notes. I'll read it to you after we eat."

Jody wasn't sure he wanted to know what was in the letter. *Things have been so great I don't want them spoiled.*

He was hungry, but he had a little trouble

swallowing at first. His throat had a lump in it that wouldn't go down. He took small bites and watched his mother's face as he chewed. *She looks okay—sort of happy. Her eyes have sparkles in them.*

When Jody's throat felt better he asked, "Do you want to leave the Blue Caboose, Mom? Will we have to move?"

"Well, that's not a problem we need to solve now. I think the three of us have to talk—get acquainted with each other again and see how we feel now. Probably all of us have changed some."

Jody took small bites of his fruit Jell-o. By this time he could swallow as well as ever. He knew why he wasn't in a hurry to finish supper. He wasn't ready to learn what his father had written. *I might not like it. I might not even believe him.*

"Come sit on the sofa," his mother said. "We'll read this letter, and then get on with our evening."

Jody watched his mother's face as she read. Sometimes tears came into her eyes, like when she read, "I've begun to feel more like a coward than if I'd deserted the army, as I was tempted to do plenty of times. Leaving you two to face things alone wouldn't win me any medals. Not even if I was the one handing them out."

Once she smiled after reading that Jody's father was having trouble sewing on buttons. "Why did that make you smile?" he asked.

"Oh, way back when you were a baby I was trying to learn to sew, trying to make a buttonhole. My thread knotted and I kept breaking it. So Barney said I wasn't giving myself room by just cutting a slit. He took the scissors and cut a hole as big as a button. By the time I made the stitches around it I had a hole as large as a silver dollar. My button was dime size."

"I guess what I remember about Dad wasn't very funny."

"What's the worst part you remember? Before he left, I mean?"

"Mainly that he yelled a lot if I made noise—or about other things, too. I got tired being quiet."

"Poor Barney. His war nightmares kept him awake so much of the time."

"I couldn't be quiet enough in here so anyone could ever sleep," Jody said.

"Well, Barney says on this last page that he's got a lot of things out of the way. Besides, three people couldn't live in here. Not for long. But we're not ready to cross that bridge yet."

Jody felt a little better. There wasn't anything in the letter that upset him more. *Except I don't want to move—but if we have to. If Mom says—*

"It's still not too cold," his mother said. "I think I'll bundle up and loop the string of Christmas lights around the rail of the mini-porch."

"I'll help," Jody said. He felt good about decorating the caboose for Christmas. *At least Mom doesn't think we'll be moving before then.*

57

Chapter 8

THE MINI-PORCH was covered with a carpet of fluffy snow. "Should we get our boots?" Jody asked.

"It's not that deep, and we won't be out here that long," his mother answered. "Here, hold this end of the string of lights." She looped the cord over the iron railing moving toward the other side. As she pulled the rubber covered extension toward the back end of the caboose she said, "I'm glad whoever put this light out here put a plug-in with it—if that's what you call it."

"Don't you know who fixed an outside light for us?" Jody asked.

"Not for sure. I asked Mr. Gable if he or someone he'd hired had put it up. But he just grinned as if he didn't know what I was talking about."

"Which means he probably did."

"Probably. Now! Ready for the lighting of the Blue Caboose?"

"It sure looks pretty," Jody said as the red, green, blue, and yellow candle-shaped bulbs glowed. "I'm going to get my boots and see how the lights look from farther away. Okay?"

"Wait on me," his mother said.

They walked out toward the street, turned, and came back.

"It's really pretty, Mom. I'm glad you thought of doing this."

A car came from behind, speeded up, and passed as they stepped to the edge of the driveway. "I keep wondering how much goes on over there at the factory at night," Jody's mother said. "Why do we see people going that way?"

"Not people, Mom. I've only seen one at a time. And then not very often."

"Well, I guess you're right. There's no use to borrow trouble—to imagine the worst."

"What do you mean *worst*?" Jody asked.

"Oh, burglars or someone snooping around to tear things up."

They stopped to take a last look at the lights before going inside. "It's like a Christmas card or a picture in a storybook," Jody's mother said.

"In a way we are living in a story by making a home in a caboose. It's like a book our teacher read a long time ago. Only those kids lived in a boxcar. And they didn't have even one parent—with them, I mean."

The sounds of the night were close. Cars over on Walnut Street seemed as near as the drive. And the rumble of a freight train at the Twelfth Street crossing could have been right behind the old factory. "Why does everything sound different, louder—but kind of—I can't think of the right word."

"I think you mean *muffled*. The snow holds all the vibrations closer to the ground. It's like a blanket above us."

"Some blanket! White and cold."

"It's not very late," Jody's mother said as she set their boots on a newspaper to absorb the melting snow. "Do you have any homework?"

"No. I finished it all at school. I really did. I'm not saying that to get out of doing it now."

"That still goes on?"

"What do you mean still? Are you saying that kids did that back in the olden times too?"

"Olden times, huh? Well, I guess some of that went on back in ages past. Anyway, I have some homework. I have some figuring to do on Mr. Gable's books."

Jody curled up on his sofa bed and looked at a Christmas gift catalog someone had left at the laundromat. *It's the same way every year,* he thought. *I see all these things and know I have to choose. It seems like I don't want anything real bad like I did other years. Is that because I'm getting older or because I know more about how much money we don't have?*

Jody was getting sleepy, but he wasn't ready to go to bed. He decided to wake himself up by making hot chocolate. He was watching marshmallows melt in both tall cups when someone pounded on the door.

Jody heard Carlos say, "Hey, Amigo, it's me," before he could open the door. "I'm all over with snow," Carlos said. "I should stay outside."

"Hey! You'll freeze. You can stand on a newspaper or take off your boots and put them beside ours."

Jody's mother smiled at Carlos as she pushed her chair back and went to the stove. "You came just in time. Look what Jody made for you to help warm you up."

Carlos talked between sips of the foamy, steaming drink. He told Jody that he and Tim had slid down the hill so many times that the snow was as slick as ice. His father had come for them when it was time to eat. "We coaxed Tim to stay. Good thing. Bueno."

What does he mean "good thing?" Jody thought. *Is Tim his best friend now?"*

"It is bueno because Tim speaks Spanish. Some he does."

"How could Tim know Spanish?" Lillian Bryant asked. "Hasn't he always lived here?"

"In this city, si. But he has not gone all the time to this school. In one place they had what is called elect—something like *elect.*"

"Probably electives. And Tim took Spanish?"

"Si. For four weeks. My mama was happy. I think she might like to have Tim help her learn some English."

"Why Tim? She hasn't wanted to be taught, has she?"

"Because she would not have to go out with strangers. She feels—how shall I say? More—more—"

"Comfortable?"

"Si. More comfortable." Carlos began to buckle his boots as they made plans to go sledding the next day. He said that Tim could come after lunch, but Tim would have to slip away from Tony, and they shouldn't expect him to come at any certain time.

Before Carlos opened the door he said, "I almost forgot what my papa told me to say. Another mobile home is to be moved in tomorrow. On your side of the drive. Up by the factory."

Lillian Bryant asked how Mr. Mendez knew they would have new neighbors and if he knew who they were. Carlos said that his father saw men digging a ditch for water lines. "Papa said if they'd waited much longer the ground would be frozen hard."

"But you don't know who they are?"

"No. Only that it is someone who works at the factory. Adios. Good night."

"Oh dear. I hope a lot of people don't decide to live over here," Jody's mother said as she picked up her pen. "But I guess I can't do anything about *that*. And I *can* work on these books."

"It seems like Mr. Gable would have told us that some other people are going to live here," Jody said before he turned the television to his favorite program.

"You're right. It doesn't seem like him not to tell us."

Jody watched one program and kept his mind on the story. Then thoughts of his father filled his mind. *It's like a tape recorder is running in my mind with memories and worries all jumbled up.* He felt he should be glad his dad was coming home. Kids were supposed to like their fathers, weren't they? What kind of a person was anyone who was glad his father was gone?

He tried to think of what he'd heard about how other kids felt about either of their parents. Tim's mother didn't really listen to his side of things. Hadn't someone said neither Tony's dad nor mom paid much attention to him? *I guess Carlos has the best feelings. He never grouches about what he's told to do or not to do. Does he feel different because he's Chicano? Are their families different from ours?*

Suddenly Jody felt sad. He had to blink to keep tears back. It hurt to think that a lot of kids couldn't, or didn't, have good feelings about their parents. Somehow he wished he knew more who had happiness in their homes.

"Mom," he said, "are you too busy to talk? It's okay if you are."

"Have I ever been too busy? Or made you feel that I was?"

"No. I didn't mean that," Jody said. "I don't remember it if you were."

"Well! Good for me. Good for both of us. What's on your mind?"

"I was just thinking I don't know many kids who have two parents who care about them."

"Oh surely there are some. There's Carlos, for one."

"I thought of him. But that's all."

"Sometimes we only hear about the bad things in life. I'm sure many of your classmates have good feelings about their homes. Why don't you listen for that kind of talk?"

"I'm luckier than some," Jody said. "I have you."

"And I have you. Honey, I think you're worried about how it will be when your father comes home. Please don't. I'll never make a decision that will make you unhappy. But don't you think we should give Barney a chance? Shouldn't we let him explain why he thought he had to leave, before we decide if we don't want to be a three-person family again?"

"I guess. But I keep being ashamed that he left us."

"I know. I've had the same feeling—worse at first than now. Think you can go to sleep now? Do you feel safe enough?"

"I feel safe enough."

"That's the way I want to keep it."

Chapter 9

JODY didn't get out of bed until after eight o'clock the next morning. His mother woke him before she went to work but told him to stay where he was as long as he liked.

When he was ready to start the day, he yawned and stretched his arms back over his head. He looked sideways and saw that the wires of the electric heater were red and glowing. He was surprised that his mother left it on. *It must be colder*, he thought as he swung his legs around and sat on the edge of the sofa bed. He listened, but no sounds came from outside—no wind, no trucks, no train whistles.

Now that he was wider awake he realized that his mother would have left a note. She wouldn't depend on him to remember what she said when he was partly asleep. He sat down at the kitchen table and read her instructions from the back of a used envelope:

1. Make toast to go with oatmeal and orange juice.
2. Put bread sacks over your socks if you go outside.
3. Don't stay out too long.
4. Turn electric heater off when you leave.
5. Sack lunch for you on top of refrigerator.
6. Be careful.

Jody turned on the television after he was dressed and watched it while he ate. *In a way I want to go sledding with Carlos, but it's so nice and warm in here that I hate to go out. I'll decide later.*

Before ten o'clock Carlos came to the door. "I must go with my father to the store. We will be gone for half an hour. When we come back we could go to the hill. Okay?"

"Okay. I'll be ready. It may take me that long to find enough clothes to keep me warm."

"Si. I know. My mama made me wear so much I feel fat. I will honk the truck horn three times when we are back."

Jody waited for Carlos' signal before he put on his warmest jacket and knit cap and gloves. When he stepped outside he saw that his mother had swept snow from the mini-porch and the steps and had even made a path out to the driveway. *I could've done that*, he thought. *Besides, the snow's not over my boot tops. Or hers either.*

When he rounded the end of the Blue Caboose he saw that a mobile home had been moved into the lot up close to the factory. It was long, and painted brown with cream around the windows and doors. A truck—or its engine and cab—was parked along the side of the drive. Two men in bright orange jackets were working at the end.

Jody felt a little shy but he wanted to know who would be their neighbors. He stopped behind the workers and said, "This where you're going to live?"

One man turned and said, "No way, kid. We're just the movers."

"You don't even know who hired you?"

"Sure we know. Big Bill, the trailer salesman hires us. What we don't know is who bought this shoebox."

Some shoebox, Jody thought as he crossed the drive. *But I guess those mobile homes do look like one.* Then he smiled inside at his own next

"Let's go," Jody said. "I get cold standing still."

68

thought. *I guess that old lady who had so many children in the nursery rhyme would have had more room in one of these than in her shoe.*

Carlos and Jody stopped to watch the men in the orange jackets work before they went to the hill. "Let's go," Jody said. "I get cold standing still."

It was cold on the hill, too. "The wind is blowing harder," Carlos said.

"I know," Jody said. "See, the snow is piling up along that fence."

"I never did hear anyone talk about snow *piles.*"

"We don't. We call them drifts—snowdrifts. Sometimes they cause a lot of trouble. Cars get stuck. Roads are closed. You ready to go?"

"Si. My face stings." Carlos asked Jody to eat with his family.

"Not this time. Mom fixed my lunch. Besides, you said Tim is coming."

"That's okay. Three can go sledding. Only I don't think I want to be out in this cold another time."

"Me neither. Come over if you want."

The men in the orange jackets, and their truck, were gone. Jody wanted to peek in the windows of the mobile home. *Someone might be living there already,* he thought. *But I'd still like to see what it's like.*

He'd passed the door when someone said, "Hey there. I saw you looking around."

"Yeah," Jody said. "You're the man who let us look around in the factory."

"Correct! Jim Hunter. Want a tour of this place?"

"Are you going to live here?"

"Me? No. No. A workman, who doubles as a watchman, is moving in—some time later. I'm just checking the furnace for him. I lived in one of these for four years. Come on in. Look around."

"Wouldn't this person care? Whoever he is?"

"I doubt it. He's a friendly guy."

Jody walked into a room that seemed like one in a house. A brown and orange striped couch set under high windows. Two chairs, one a gold rocker and another a tan swivel chair, set at either end. He saw a television and a bookshelf and two tables with tall lamps with light tan shades.

"This is really neat. And that kitchen is like one in a house—better than my mom has ever had."

"Go on down the hall. Peek in the bathroom and the two other rooms."

"I never thought there'd be so much room and so many closets and drawers. Does this man have a family?"

Mr. Hunter didn't answer and Jody was ready to repeat the question. He saw that the factory manager was bending over the range in the kitchen. Without raising up he said, "Yeah, he

71

has a family. But he doesn't know when they'll be coming here."

Jody was about to ask about the ages of the new neighbor's children, if he had any. Mr. Hunter seemed to read his mind. "As far as I know, there's a boy about your age." As they stepped down from the black metal steps he kept talking. "You and your mama keeping warm over there?"

"We're doing fine," Jody said. "Thanks."

The wind was strong from the north and Jody had to push to shut the caboose door. He could feel cold air coming around the cracks. He remembered that his mother tacked a blanket over the windows when they lived in the apartment. The caboose wasn't as warm as usual and Jody wished he'd asked if he could use the electric heater. *But I'm not supposed to,* he thought, as he turned the knob on the television. He took his sack lunch to his mother's rocking chair after taking a folded blanket from under his bed.

He was warm as he ate two ham salad sandwiches, peeled a tangerine, and munched on three oatmeal cookies. He was thirsty and wished he'd poured a glass of water or milk while he was up. *But I'm so warm I hate to move.*

His eyelids kept closing and he couldn't keep track of the television program. He curled up on his bed, pulling the blanket over his shoulders. *I hope Mom doesn't have a hard time getting home,* he thought.

He woke with a rush of cold air coming into the room. "Jody," his mother called, "you are here?"

"Sure, Mom. Is it four-thirty already?"

"No, only two. Mr. Gable sent me home when he heard the storm warnings. Some snow, colder temperatures, and high winds are to keep up most of the night. Not many people are out. Only two brought laundry since noon. So we closed."

Jody saw two sacks of groceries and two large cardboard boxes inside the door. "Did you carry all that stuff?"

"Oh no. Mr. Gable brought me in the truck. I couldn't have carried the electric blankets. The boxes would probably have been like sails— blown me across the place."

"Did you buy the blankets?"

"No. The Gables have seven. Their children, who live in California, keep sending them at Christmas. Mrs. Gable says they think we always have ice and snow. We're only borrowing them. For now, anyway."

She plugged in the heater and tacked a piece of plastic across the door. The caboose was soon warmer, but the wind whistled and puffed.

Jody offered to fry hamburgers while his mother heated pork and beans and sliced to-matoes. "I think we can keep warm okay, don't you, Mom?" Jody said as he sat down across from her at the table.

"Well, we're giving ourselves a good chance to find out, aren't we? So far, so good. Right, son?"

"Right."

The wind kept blowing and sometimes Jody thought the Blue Caboose trembled a little. *But like Mom said once, it's been here a long, long time. It hasn't blown away yet.*

After the dishes were washed and put away Jody sat on the sofa bed with one electric blanket for a cover. His mother spread the other around her shoulders and over her knees as she rocked.

"These are nice," she said. "We might buy them from Mrs. Gable. I think she'd give them to me if I'd let her."

They watched television until nine-thirty, until someone pounded on the back door.

"Who could be out on a night like this?" his mother said.

"Don't open it until you find out, Mom. That's what you always tell me."

"I won't." Jody saw his mother take a deep breath as she walked to the back of the caboose and asked, "Who's there?"

Jody heard a man's voice but couldn't tell what he said. His mother turned. "Jody, honey. It's your father."

Chapter 10

JODY'S HEART beat faster. He felt like covering his head, turning his face to the wall. But he didn't. He listened.

"Could I come in Lilly Ann?" the man said. Jody knew it was his dad, but it had been so long since he'd heard him talk that the voice was like that of a stranger.

"Of course," Jody's mother said. "I mean, I'm surprised to see you. When did you get back?"

"That will take some explaining. But something else needs to be said first. This storm is going to get worse before it gets better. The winds are fierce. Are you having trouble keeping warm?"

"A little," Jody's mother said. "It's chilly around the edges. The electric blankets help."

"To get to the point," Barney Bryant said, "I want you to move."

Jody spoke for the first time since his dad had come through the door. "Move! Where?"

"I have some idea of how you feel about the caboose. And about me. But those feelings are not the same. They don't quite match up. I'd like for both of you to listen."

"Go ahead," Lillian Bryant said. "Jody and I have talked. We agreed that we should give you a chance to explain."

"If you mean why I left you stranded, that will have to come later. I own—or partly own—that mobile home, the one that we got moved in down toward the factory. You'll be warmer there, safer maybe. I want you to go over there at least until the storm passes. I don't need to stay there. I can bundle up here."

"Do you think this is wise?"

"I know it is."

Jody knew it was his dad, but it had been so long since he'd heard him talk that the voice was like that of a stranger.

76

Jody watched his mother's face as she sat down on his sofa bed. "I think we should go for now. Can you trust me to know what I think's best?"

"I trust you, Mom, even if I don't want to leave here."

"Then get dressed. Gather up your schoolwork and I'll put some of our extra food in a basket."

"That might be a good idea," Jody's father said. "I'm not too well stocked up."

As Jody put on his boots his thoughts seemed to go two ways. He didn't feel easy or right about going. Did his dad think he could come back and order them around? Did he have the right to do that—after skipping out? *But that mobile home was really neat. And Mom thinks we'll be safer,* he thought. *I guess she was a little scared, but she didn't let on.*

"We best leave the electric heater on—try to keep water pipes from freezing," Barney Bryant said. "But I'll turn out this oil stove heater." He raised up. "It's this heater that made up my mind to try to get you to move. A small heater's not too good if your room doesn't have good air circulation."

"Well, the wind sort of puffs down the chimney. And we have a lot of circulation from air coming around the cracks," Lillian Bryant said. "Got everything you want to take, Jody?"

"I about forgot," Jody's father said. "I don't have enough covers for three beds. Could we take the electric blankets?"

"Better roll them into a bundle," Lillian Bryant said. "That way they'll be easier to carry in the wind."

"I'll lead the way. You walk in my boot tracks," Jody's father said.

The wind and the cold took Jody's breath. *It's like I swallowed a big chunk of winter,* he thought. He noticed that the snow was deeper than it had been before dark. *It would be over my boot tops if Dad hadn't made a kind of path.* He stood against the side of the mobile home, to be out of the wind a little, while his father unlocked the door and his mother went up the black iron steps. Then he took a deep breath as he thought, *Might as well get this over with. I can't stay out here all night.* But he had the strong feeling that he'd like to turn around and go back to the Blue Caboose. *I know how I feel when I'm there.*

"This is nice," Lillian Bryant said. "And warm."

"Well, make yourselves at home if you can. You can pick out your own bedrooms. I'll bunk on this couch, or go over to the caboose."

Jody took the end room. He knew that wind kept his mother awake and it wouldn't be as strong in the middle. "We'll plug in the blankets now," she said, "and our beds will be as warm as toast."

"I'd as soon go to bed right now," Jody said. *I'm not that sleepy,* he thought, *but I'm mixed up about my feelings and how to act with Dad.*

"I know. We're all a little uneasy with each other."

Jody started to say that he wasn't uneasy with her. Then he shook his head and turned away. *But I'm even a little uneasy with Mom,* he thought. *It's not like it was when we were by ourselves.*

He followed his mother to the living room. "Got a favorite television program, Jody?" his father asked.

"Sort of."

"Before we turn it on I'd like some answers," Lillian Bryant said. "First, when did you get back?"

Barney scratched his head with one finger. "You're not going to believe this, Lilly Ann. But I've been in Muncie nearly two and a half months now."

Did he call Mom Lilly Ann before he went away? Jody thought. *I don't remember.*

"That is hard to believe. You must have kept yourself to another part of town."

"No, I've been right here. I've had my eye on you more or less. To make a long story short, I'm sort of a designer and a combination of night watchman and tool operator at the factory." He said that he'd kept in touch with Joe Gable. "He told me that business was getting better. And they were needing ideas for new wooden products. So he told them about my whittling. One thing led to the other and I got the job."

80

"Where did you live?" Jody's mother asked.

"In the loft. We boarded up a corner, which was alright until this month."

"Looks like we'd have seen you," Jody said.

"You nearly did, more than once. One day you and your friend were looking around. I started down the ladder and scooted right up again."

"I didn't see you. Carlos did."

"I don't understand why you didn't want—" Lillian Bryant said. Then she stopped. "Yes, I do. I think. You were trying to prove that you could hold a job."

"You've hit the nail on the head. And when this place opened up, I thought it'd be a way to sort of stand by in the meantime."

"I guess there's a lot more we could talk about but it's getting late," Jody's mother said. "Does hot chocolate sound good to anyone besides me? I brought some along—and even paper cups."

Jody held up his hand, a signal he and his mother often gave. He glanced at his dad and he was doing the same. Had he done that before? *I don't know. It's like the time he was with us is in pieces.*

"Are you sure this mobile home won't blow over?" Lillian said as she stirred chocolate powder into the warming milk. "You read about that happening."

"Some of the men from the factory helped me tie it down. That's why I didn't get out to get more food."

"I didn't see you out there."

"That's because we worked after dark. We nearly froze."

"Were you sure we'd come?"

"No, but I knew I had to ask you after I heard the weather bulletin about the winter storm warning."

Jody listened while his mom and dad talked. So far no one sounded mad. *I'm not sure if that's how I want it to be.*

"I don't think I'll watch television, Mom," he said. "I couldn't hold my eyes open until the program is over. No use to start a story then have to wonder how it came out. Okay if I go to bed?"

"Sure is. I'll go, too. I know what you're thinking, Barney, that we have a lot to talk about. But I made the mistake of keeping things from Jody when you left—how I felt, I mean. I don't want to do that to him again."

"Don't worry, Lilly Ann. Hurts don't heal overnight. If you're bothered, I can sleep in the caboose like I said."

"No need to do that."

Jody's mother came into the end bedroom before he went to sleep. "You warm, honey?"

"Sure. Like you said, warm as toast."

"You still feel uneasy about being here?"

"Well, not as much. I mean, Dad didn't try to hug me or make excuses or anything."

"I know. I believe him. He just wanted us to be safe. Good night, Jody. Oh, my goodness! You

82

know what I forgot to do before we left the Blue Caboose?"

"Mom, you're not going back tonight?"

"No, I guess it won't hurt for the Christmas lights on the mini-porch to burn all night. They could blow away or burn out but it's too cold for me to do anything about that now."

Jody could hear the sound of the television. It was faint and faraway. He thought of Carlos and hoped the Mendez family was as warm as he was. *Carlos would sure be surprised if he knew where I am. Would he say this is bueno?*

Questions raced through his mind but he was too sleepy to think about answers. *Besides, I wouldn't know all of them.* He thought of the Blue Caboose. Was the snow blowing so hard that no one could see the red, green, blue, and yellow lights? *I can see it in my mind. That is bueno.*

Jody turned over and pulled the warm, gold blanket over his ear to shut out the whistle and the whish of the cold winter wind.

Chapter 11

WHEN JODY opened his eyes the next morning, he looked around and blinked. *It's like I'm in a dream. Where am I?* The things that had happened the day before began to come back to him in pieces, like parts of a puzzle.

He raised up on one elbow and listened. There was stillness both inside and outside the mobile home. The wind had stopped blowing; there was no whishing or whistling. No one was talking.

Has Mom gone to work? he thought. *Has she left me here with Dad? Is he here?*

He took the five steps needed to get to the hallway and then tiptoed toward the living room. *If I see Dad, I'll go back to bed and act like I'm asleep.* He stopped as he saw his mother come around the half wall that separated the living room and kitchen.

"Good morning, Jody," she said. "I see you decided not to sleep all day."

"Is it real late?"

"Late for us, almost nine-thirty."

"Aren't you going to work?" Jody asked. "Oh, I forgot. It's Sunday. Are we here by ourselves?"

"Yes. Your father said he had to check on some things over at the factory."

"But I guess he'll come back here to eat—and sleep."

"He says not. He thinks we all need time to see if our lives can fit back together. He'll stay in the caboose. He took one of the electric blankets with him. And as you very well know there's plenty of food over there. More than here—right now anyway."

Jody turned the television knob but decided there wasn't anything that he wanted to see. He went to the kitchen and sat down on one side of the booth and looked out the wide window. Snow covered all the ground he could see and in some places the drifts were like ridged hills. "Is it too cold to play out?" he asked.

"Yes, I'm afraid it is. The thermometer says ten degrees below zero. You could get frostbite in a little while in weather like this. You don't know what to do with yourself—right?"

"Right. I could see if Carlos wants to come here. It's not too cold to go that far, is it?"

"No. And ask if he can stay and eat with us."

Jody didn't move from the booth. He leaned his head on his arms which he folded on the table. He looked sideways and watched two gray-brown birds hop across the snow. *Looks like their feet would freeze*, he thought. *Do birds get frostbite?*

He wanted to have Carlos over in one way and in one way he didn't. He knew he'd have to do a lot of explaining. Carlos would ask a bunch of questions about his dad, when he came back, and if all of them were going to live in the mobile home as a family. *I know what he'd say. Bueno. Well, I'm not so sure about it being that good.*

As he watched, Carlos crossed the stone driveway going in the direction of the Blue Caboose. Jody slipped out of the booth, hurried to the door, and yelled, "Hey, Amigo. I'm here."

Jody stepped back inside, out of the cold, and waited to open the door for Carlos. He could see his friend stomping through the deep snow, lifting his knees high to get from one deep stepping place to the next.

"I didn't know you would be living in your papa's new home so soon," Carlos said. "This is bueno—*bueno-good.*"

"How did you know about my dad and about him buying this place? But first take off your coat, your boots, and stuff."

Carlos talked as he unzipped and unbuckled his two jackets and boots. "My papa told me last night. He saw yours—your dad, go over to the caboose."

"But how did Mr. Mendez know who Barney was?" Lillian Bryant asked.

"He has known that for many weeks. But I didn't. Mr. Gable told him. He said Senor Bryant would be living in the factory. He told Papa not to be surprised if he saw someone coming and going when no one else was working."

Lillian Bryant said, "Mr. Gable has known a lot. I'm sure that he's had much to do with Barney being here."

"Is your papa here?" Carlos asked.

"No, he's over at the factory."

Jody's mother asked Carlos to spend the day with them.

"I have to ask," Carlos said. "We did not go to the big church today. Papa's truck would not go."

"And we didn't walk to the little one over on Gharkey," Jody's mother said.

Jody led Carlos through the trailer before they went to the Mendez mobile home. On the way back Carlos said, "Having snow is not all bueno. It would be better if it was warm."

"If it was warm we wouldn't have snow."

"I know."

They folded paper into birds and Christmas tree ornaments as they'd learned to do in school. Jody was sailing his yellow paper bird when someone knocked on the door.

"I'll get it, Mom," Jody said. He stepped back when he saw his father on the black iron steps.

"I can't come in. I have to fire the furnace. Here, I brought you a lunch." As Jody took the big white and red bag he said, "Wow. Fried chicken. Thanks."

"Chicken and the works. I see you have a visitor. Hi, Carlos," Barney Bryant said.

"How'd you know my name?"

"I see you around. I heard Jody call you a few times."

By this time Lillian Bryant had reached the living room. "Can't you stay and eat with us?"

"Not this time. I have my sack in the truck. And the coffee pot's on the hot plate at the factory."

After the chicken was reheated in the oven Jody and his mother and Carlos sat in the booth and ate and talked for over an hour. Carlos talked about the places he'd been every year before the Mendez family left the migrant stream. "That is called 'settling out,'" he said.

He said that they used to leave Texas in the spring or early summer every year. They'd move north from state to state as the different crops were ready to harvest.

"We picked strawberries in Tennessee, dug potatoes in Alabama, picked cherries in Michigan, and tomatoes here in Indiana," Carlos said. "Sometimes we went to Florida when oranges, grapefruit, cabbage, and lettuce needed to be picked. Then we went back to Texas until another spring and started all over again."

"I wouldn't like all that moving," Jody said.

"I didn't either. Sometimes I didn't know the name of the town where we were. There were so many places to remember. But this last move was to a better place."

The boys watched a football game until Mr. Mendez came to the door. "Senora. My truck will run now. I'm going to the store for food. Is there anything you will need?"

"Yes, there is," Lillian Bryant said. "It looks like we'll be here another night at least. Is it getting colder?"

"Si. The sun is down."

"I'll make a list. Jody, would you like to go and pick up the things we need? Is that alright with you Mr. Mendez?"

"Si. And Carlos can help me find what his mama wants."

Jody found the hot dogs, buns, eggs, milk, and bread and waited at the front of the store until Carlos and his father went through the check-out line.

Someone grabbed his arm and Tim said, "How'd you get here?"

"I came with them. Carlos and his dad."

"I see. I'm going to ask them if I can go home with them."

"Why? I mean should you?"

"They won't care. I didn't get over to help Mrs. Mendez with her English."

"Won't your mama care?" Mr. Mendez asked as they left.

"She's not home. She went over where Dad got a job. I don't know when she'll get back."

"I'll walk from here," Jody said as they were about to pass the Mendez home. "I don't have much to carry. See you."

He walked slowly until Tim was inside. "No need for him to know I'm not going to the caboose. No need to have him ask a bunch of questions."

He glanced toward his caboose home. The Christmas tree lights were not shining in the early darkness of the winter evening. Did they burn out? Or had his father unplugged them?

He hurried up the drive. All at once he was hungry. "And I know what we're going to have. I have our supper—hot dogs and buns—and milk for hot chocolate maybe."

The tall lamps made circles of light in the living room. Jody was thinking that it was good to be where it was new and warm. Then he looked toward the kitchen, and stopped. His father was sitting in the booth.

Chapter 12

JODY put the sack of groceries on the peach-colored cabinet. He didn't know what to say or do. *I guess I can't run away forever,* he thought.

"Want your hot dogs boiled or roasted under the broiler?" his mother asked.

"You know, Mom. Roasted, always."

"I'm frying some potatoes."

"That was my doing," Jody's father said. "It's been a month of Sundays—or maybe longer, since I've had plain skillet fried potatoes."

Jody was ready to ask his mother to make them crusty when his father added, "And I also put in a request that some be brown and crusty."

Are Dad and I alike in some ways? Jody thought. *I don't know. I never thought before if I was like him or not. Why didn't Mom ever say that we were?* He'd heard people say that some kids were just like their dads. No one ever had compared him to his father. At least not when he heard them.

"You'd better scrub your hands," Jody's mother said. "These potatoes will be done in a jiffy. And don't ask how long a jiffy is."

"Because you don't know."

"Because I don't know."

As Jody turned to go down the hall to the bathroom he saw his father's face. He was smiling and Jody was almost sure he saw tears in his dad's eyes. Why would that be?

He took his coat to the room at the end of the hall. *I have to admit it's nice in here,* he thought. *It's sort of a private place. You couldn't have that in a one-room home.*

He shook his head. *I still don't want to leave the Blue Caboose. I like it there.*

His father scooted over and Jody sat down on the same side of the booth, as close to the end as he could get. He listened as his parents talked. Lillian Bryant asked what Barney did for the new factory.

"Mostly—or the best part—is designing new wood products. Right now I'm working on two items, a rack for spices and a set of wall plaques of Snoopy characters." He went on to say that he was night watchman for five nights of the week and in his free time he operated a saw.

"You like it there, don't you?"

"Better than anything I've ever tried. And as you know, I tried a passel of things."

What's a passel? Jody thought. *Something like a big bunch?*

Barney went on to say that he thought the new business in the old factory would succeed. "Jim Hunter's a top-notch manager and all of us like what we're doing."

"Perhaps there's another reason," Lillian said. "The business was started for a good reason. The people in the church where Jody and I have been going saw a way to help others."

"Could be you're right," Barney said. "Do you think you two are ready to talk to me about my ducking out?"

Oh no, Jody thought, *Here it comes!*

"We can make a start," Lillian said. "Shouldn't we wait until I do the dishes?"

"I'll have to be at the factory by seven. That gives us nearly an hour, which may be about as long as any of us can stand talking about our painful past."

Jody sat near his mother on the soft couch and his father faced them from the swivel rocker. He drummed his fingers on the wooden end of the chair arm. *I guess he's uneasy too*, Jody thought.

"I been thinking a lot about what I'd say. I could fill a book—or a whole set of them with the stuff that went through my mind. But I think I'll get to the heart of the matter. I'll just tell why I left, why I couldn't stand to stay."

"Was it us?" Lillian asked. "Did we make things hard for you? Did I?"

"No, not by anything you did or said." Jody's father talked for ten minutes. Jody kept his eyes on the clock all the time and watched one number fall out of sight and another click into its place.

"There's a lot about war I'd as soon not remember," Barney said. "But that's a part of this sad story." He said that he saw so much killing and wounding in Vietnam that he often thought of deserting but didn't want to spend his life in a faraway land. He said he'd kicked himself over and over for not sticking at some job, for thinking that enlisting would be best.

"And you know about the nightmares I had—the yelling and the nights without sleep. But you can't know what I saw in my mind that caused the nightmares. I don't want you ever to know."

"Is that why you left? To try to get away from the nightmares?"

"No. I didn't get away from them by running. But they're fading away. No, it was seeing Jody grow up that I couldn't bear."

"Me? What did I—"

"No Jody—you didn't do anything. It was this way. I saw young men—boys to me—killed or torn up. And when I got back and saw you nearly a foot taller than when I went away, I couldn't face the fact that the same thing could happen to you. I didn't want to get close to you, and then be hurt."

"Couldn't you have talked to me about this?" Lillian asked.

"I thought of it. I nearly burst trying to hold the words in. But I didn't want to put the same fear in your mind. Can you understand this feeling, Jody?"

"I think so. A little."

"Then, since you felt so strongly, why did you come back?"

Barney leaned his head back on the chair and smiled for the first time since he'd started the explanation. "It was you two. Moving into the caboose. Making a home for yourselves. The clincher, the deciding point, came when I heard that you'd painted the railing on the back platform gold."

"We call that the mini-porch, Dad."

"Okay. The mini-porch."

"But I don't understand how you knew what we were doing," Lillian said. "I never wrote. You never gave me an address. And the postmarks were so blurred that I didn't know what town or even what state you were in."

"Lilly Ann. When those letters were smudged

it was done by Joe Gable's thumb. They were mailed right here in Muncie *after* I came back."

"I'm beginning to see the light," Lillian said. "Mr. Gable has been a big part of what has happened."

"He has. He sure has. I called him after I got my first job, working in an orange grove in Florida. I had plenty of Vitamin C down there."

Barney explained that Mr. Gable hadn't been easy on him for leaving his family, but had offered to help. "He wrote to me, called me twice, and when the factory job opened up he put in a good word for me. Only at the time I thought his faith in me might not ever be proven. Anyway, that's why I left and how I got back. And now it's time to get on the job. I'll check in tomorrow."

"You're staying in the caboose tonight?"

"No, I'll keep an eye on things at the factory until daylight then catch a few hours sleep in the caboose. I work in shifts and sleep the same way. That suits me fine. See you."

"See you, Dad."

Jody stayed on the couch after his mother went to the kitchen. He thought about some of the things he'd heard. *I guess I don't understand how Dad felt, not all the way. But I'm not as mad as I was.*

"Don't you have some homework to do?" his mother asked.

"Yeah, a little." He went to the room at the end of the hall and took his social studies book to the booth in the kitchen. He worked until his mother finished the dishes, then he joined her in the living room. "Okay if I watch television?"

"Let's do."

Neither Jody nor his mother brought up the subject of what his father had said until they started down the hall on the way to bed. They'd watched two programs, drank hot tea, and ate slices of cinnamon toast. After the television was off Jody could hear the click and the sputter as the gas furnace clicked on and flared into a brighter flame.

"You feel any different about your dad than you did?" Jody's mother asked as she stopped at the door of the middle room.

"Some, but I don't know for sure. Why?"

"I know. Like I said, we have a lot of thinking and more talking to do."

"Talking about what, Mom?" Jody asked.

"Oh, things like me working and us going to church. I'd not stop either of those. They're part of our life now. Real good parts—which I like. I'm glad Barney's not pushing us."

"Me too. 'Night, Mom."

Jody didn't go to sleep until after the night train crossed Twelfth Street. He folded his hands behind his head and looked out the high window. He could see the milky light from the pole at the edge of the factory parking lot. He thought of Carlos and wondered how long Tim had stayed in the Mendez mobile home. Would Tim become

Carlos' best friend? *I don't think it'll be any different with Carlos and me. I don't think it will.*

He thought of Mr. Gable trying to help his dad and of all the kind things the tall man had done for him and his mother. *Seems like a lot of good can go on without us knowing anything about it,* he thought. He felt warm and safe as he let his eyes close and pulled the electric blanket over his shoulders.

Chapter 13

JODY'S father came to the mobile home the next morning. "Time for school," he said. "Better let me taxi you over, you and Carlos. I took one passenger already—your mother."

"I didn't hear you."

"I know. I picked her up down the drive. You'd better zip up that jacket. It's still cold."

As his father locked the door behind them, Jody asked, "How'd you know it was time for me to leave for school?"

"Like I said, I've had my eye on you."

As Jody and Carlos hurried up the walk into Riley School, Carlos asked, "Is it a good thing for you that your papa is back?"

"Well, it's better than I thought it might be. I guess you can't understand how it could be bad. You don't know how it was."

"No, I've never lived where my papa wasn't with us."

After school the boys went to the laundromat. Frost covered most of the glass of the front windows. The steam from the washers and dryers made moisture that froze into designs. "They are like leaves and flowers," Carlos said. "White and icy."

Mr. Mendez came to pick them up. "I say to Senor Bryant we will take turns while it is so cold. And I am to tell you that some food from the caboose is now in the mobile home."

On the way up the driveway Lillian Bryant said, "Would you like to stay all night with us, Carlos? In the caboose there wasn't sleeping room. Even if you slept toe-to-toe you'd have needed to pull your knees up. What do you say, Mr. Mendez?"

"We will talk to his mama and Carlos will tell you yes or no."

It was a good evening for Jody. He thought once or twice that his father might come, but that didn't upset him. It didn't spoil the fun of having a friend stay overnight.

It was three days before Barney Bryant came to the mobile home again. The weather was warmer. The snow had melted from the driveway but not from the grassy places. Drifts were lower but not gone. Jody opened the door and said, "Hi."

"Hi, yourself. I stopped by the Swish and the Slosh, as Joe calls it. I asked Lilly Ann if she'd like to go with us to eat out."

"Us?"

"Yes, you and me. Are you in the mood?"

"I'm in the mood. Should I dress up?"

"You look fine to me. Real fine." For the first time since he came back, Jody's father reached out to touch him. Jody didn't move away from the hand on his shoulder. He didn't want to.

"Then I'll be here at 5:30, after I put the factory furnace to bed for another four hours."

As they left the factory lot Barney Bryant asked, "Who wants to go where?"

"You didn't have a place in mind?" Jody's mother asked.

"No, just getting you to go was the main idea."

"It didn't take too much coaxing, did it?"

"No, it didn't. You surprised me."

"Any suggestions, Jody?" his mother asked.

"You decide, Mom. You know me. Any place where they have cheeseburgers and french fries is okay by me."

They ate in a cafeteria on the north side of town. The tables were near a fireplace and Jody watched the flames curl around the logs. *It's like they are fingers of fire,* he thought.

His parents talked and Jody mostly listened. Before they left, many pieces of the puzzle seemed to fit together. His mother asked if the Blue Caboose was warmer now that the wind wasn't strong.

"Yes," Barney said. "But it wouldn't be if I hadn't stored the bales of straw beneath it and fenced them in with boards."

"Then it was you who did that. I kept trying to give Mr. Gable the credit for that."

"And what did Joe say?"

"Oh, you know him. He just grinned, shoved his hat back on his head, and acted like he didn't know what I was talking about."

"Still have an empty corner somewhere, Jody? Do you have room for dessert maybe?" his father asked.

"Well, you and mom talked so long that I might squeeze in a piece of that strawberry pie."

"Good idea. I'll have some too. How about you, Lilly Ann?"

"If they'll let me have half a slice, I'll join you."

Before they were ready to leave Lillian Bryant said, "A remark of yours keeps puzzling me, Barney. Why did my painting the mini-porch

His parents talked and Jody mostly listened. Before they left, many pieces of the puzzle seemed to fit together.

gold have anything to do with your decision to come back?"

Barney smiled and nodded. "I can see how that might be hard for you to understand." He explained that after he heard about the gold paint he remembered other things, and other times. There was the time when Lillian had worked for hours stenciling a border of roses on the ends of Jody's first bed, one they'd bought at a secondhand store. "And wherever we lived, in every crummy place, you planted flowers in those boxes we lugged from one place to the other."

"And—how did that influence you?"

"Well, all at once I realized how brave you always are. And—on the other side of the coin—I saw myself as an A-1 quitter. I didn't like that picture. Do you think I can change it, Lilly Ann? Do you have any faith left in me?"

Jody looked at his mother. Tears were filling her eyes. His own felt wet too.

"I believe you truly are trying. That's what I believe."

"That's enough for now. The proving is up to me. Everyone ready to move on?"

They stopped at the shopping center on the way across town. Jody needed some new gym shoes and both branches of the Bryant family needed milk. When Lillian opened her purse in the shoe store Barney said, "It's my turn to pay. In fact I have a lot of catching up to do."

As they turned onto Walnut Street Jody's mother said, "Aren't you ready to move back into your place? To exchange places again?"

Jody could see his father's face in the glow of the truck's dash lights. *I know what he's going to say.*

"No, this is your home. Maybe you'd like it better in another location. That can be taken care of later."

"What's wrong with the location? We like it here."

As Barney Bryant turned the ignition key he said, "I have another half hour. Could we talk?"

Lillian hung her coat in a hall closet and came back to the couch to listen. Jody sat in the swivel rocker, turning it a little, first one way then the other.

"I'd like more than anything I ever thought of wanting—or hoped to have—for us to live together as a family again," Jody's father said. "But this has to be right or not at all. It's for the three of us to decide."

"I feel the same way," Jody's mother said.

"The thing is, Lilly Ann, do you think we're getting closer? Nearer to being easy with each other?"

"Oh yes, I do. Jody and I have talked about that. And one more thing, I agree that we're going about this in the best way. No pushing. No pressure. Only I do feel this is your mobile home."

"It's ours. And don't worry about my being in the caboose. If it was good enough for you, it's for sure good enough for me. By the way, I have an idea about that caboose, Jody. You think it over. If the time comes when we all live in the mobile home the caboose could be a kind of clubhouse, a playroom for you and Carlos."

Jody did like the idea. "There's not a lot of room to play here. Or where the Mendez family is," he said.

"That's what I thought," Barney said. "And I'm making you a Christmas present, a fun type that wouldn't fit here. How'd you feel about this, Lilly Ann, if the time comes?"

"It sounds fine to me. Of course we'd have to set up rules. About lighting the stove and not letting too many in at a time."

"Sure. Well, I must go. But before I do, I have your Christmas tree lights in the truck. The wind was about to whip them to pieces."

"We could put them around the railing here," Jody's mother said. "And that makes me think. We will have more room for a tree here, one that's a little taller." She told Barney that she and Jody had planned to string cranberries and popcorn, for an old-fashioned tree.

"Only we need lights, red and white."

"Then we'll get that done," Barney said.

After his father left, Jody followed his mother to the kitchen. She sat down across from him in the booth.

"You know, Mom, Dad's a lot different than the way I mostly remember him."

"I know how that could be for you. But it's the other way with me. He's now mostly, as you put it, how he was before the war."

"I guess you liked him an awful lot?" Jody said.

"Yes, I did. And I'm finding out I still do. Now that the hurt is healed—almost gone. Do you think you'd be unhappy if he moved in with us?"

"No. I guess we could keep on getting to know each other."

"We probably should keep on living as we are until being together seems right to all of us. Like Carlos said, some moves can be to better places."

"I was thinking, Mom," Jody said. "Christmas might be a good time for this to be home for all of us."

"That's a good idea. You'd be getting your dad back for Christmas."

"He probably wouldn't fit under our cranberry and popcorn tree. But I guess he'd be an okay present. Yes, I believe I'd like that."

Dorothy Hamilton, a homemaker from Selma, Indiana, began writing books after she became a grandmother. As a private tutor, she has helped hundreds of students with learning difficulties. Many of her books reflect the hurts she observed in her students. She offers hope to others in similar circumstances.

Mindy is caught in the middle of her parents' divorce. *Charco* and his family live on unemployment checks. *Jason* would like to attend a trade school but his parents want him to go to college.

Other titles include: *Amanda Fair* (shoplifting), *Anita's Choice* (migrant workers), *Bittersweet Days* (snobbery at school), *The Blue Caboose* and *Winter Caboose* (an absent father), *Busboys at Big Bend* (Mexican-American friendship), *The Castle* (friendship with the very rich), *Christmas for Holly* and *Holly's New Year* (a foster child), *Cricket* (a pony story), *Eric's Discovery* (vandalism), *The Gift of a*

Home (problems of becoming rich), and *Gina In-Between* (accepting her widowed mother's boyfriend).

Mrs. Hamilton is also author of *Jim Musco* (a Delaware Indian boy), *Ken's Hideout* (his father died) and *Ken's Bright Room* (a sequel), *Kerry* (growing up), *Last One Chosen* (a handicapped boy), *Linda's Rain Tree* (a black girl), *Mari's Mountain* (a runaway girl), *Neva's Patchwork Pillow* (Appalachia), *Rosalie* and *Rosalie at Eleven* (life in grandma's day), *Scamp and the Blizzard Boys* (friendship in a winter storm), *Straight Mark* (drugs), *Tony Savala* (a Basque boy), and *Winter Girl* (jealousy).

Four books of adult fiction by Mrs. Hamilton are also available: *Settled Furrows* and a trilogy on family relationships, *The Killdeer, The Quail,* and *The Eagle.*

In addition to writing, Mrs. Hamilton has spoken to more than 300,000 students in over 560 schools in five states, Canada, and 48 counties of Indiana.

"What's your favorite part in writing a book?" one young student asked.

"Right now, it's being here with you," she replied.

"The prospect of facing 80 fifth- and sixth-graders at the same time is enough to send many adults for the nearest exit," a news reporter noted, "but for Dorothy Hamilton it is pure delight."

Date Due